THE ZACK FILES

Tell a Lie and Your Butt Will Grow

LETTERS TO DAN GREENBURG
ABOUT THE ZACK FILES:

From a mother in New York, NY: "Just wanted to let you know that it was THE ZACK FILES that made my son discover the joy of reading...I tried everything to get him interested...THE ZACK FILES turned my son into a reader overnight. Now he complains when he's out of books!"

From a boy named Toby in New York, NY: "The reason why I like your books is because you explain things that no other writer would even dream of explaining to kids."

From Tara in Floral Park, NY: "When I read your books I felt like I was in the book with you. We love your books!"

From a teacher in West Chester, PA: "I cannot thank you enough for writing such a fantastic series."

From Max in Old Bridge, NJ: "I wasn't such a great reader until I discovered your books."

From Monica in Burbank, IL: "I read almost all of your books and I loved the ones I read. I'm a big fan! *I'm Out of My Body, Please Leave a Message*. That's a funny title. It makes me think of it being the best book in the world."

From three mothers in Toronto: "You have managed to take three boys and unlock the world of reading. In January they could best be characterized as boys who 'read only under duress.' Now these same guys are similar in that they are motivated to READ."

From Stephanie in Hastings, NY: "If someone didn't like your books that would be crazy."

From Dana in Floral Park, NY: "I really LOVE I mean LOVE your books. I read them a million times. I wish I could buy more. They are so good and so funny."

From a teacher in Pelham, NH: "My students are thoroughly enjoying [THE ZACK FILES]. Some are reading a book a night."

From Madeleine in Hastings, NY: "I love your books...I hope you keep making many more Zack Files."

THE ZACK FILES ™

Tell a Lie and Your Butt Will Grow

By Dan Greenburg

Illustrated by Jack E. Davis

GROSSET & DUNLAP • NEW YORK

For Judith, and for the real Zack,
with love—D.G.

I'd like to thank my editor
Jane O'Connor, who makes the process
of writing and revising so much fun,
and without whom
these books would not exist.

I also want to thank
Emily Sollinger and Megan Bryant
for their terrific ideas.

Text copyright © 2002 by Dan Greenburg. Illustrations copyright © 2002 by Jack E. Davis.
All rights reserved. Published by Grosset & Dunlap, a division of Penguin Putnam Books
for Young Readers, 345 Hudson Street, New York, NY 10014. GROSSET & DUNLAP and
THE ZACK FILES are trademarks of Penguin Putnam Inc. Published simultaneously in
Canada. Printed in the U.S.A.

Library of Congress Cataloging-in-Publication Data is available.

ISBN 0-448-42682-X   D   E   F   G   H   I   J

Chapter 1

Here are three things I hate:

(1) Eating a cookie you thought was chocolate chip and finding out the chocolate chip is a beetle.

(2) Going to the bathroom in the school john and finding out that other kids have stolen the toilet paper from your stall.

(3) Kids who aren't impressed that you actually handled a real baby alligator and who lie and tell you they did something a whole lot cooler and braver.

OK, I'm probably getting a little ahead of myself.

My name is Zack. I'm ten and a half. I'm in the fifth grade at the Horace Hyde-White School for Boys. That's in New York City. My parents are divorced. Did I mention that? Well, anyway, they are. I spend about half my time with each of them, but it's when I'm with my dad that really weird things happen to me.

Like this time I'm going to tell you about.

Dad had taken me to a travel fair at the Javits Convention Center. They had people from all over the world trying to get you to visit their countries. There were exhibits from almost everywhere you could think of: Egypt, Israel, Minneapolis, Poland, the Florida Everglades.

The Florida Everglades exhibit was my favorite because they had baby alligators that were about a foot long. You know how baby animals always look so cute? Well, baby alligators aren't cute. They look at you like they'd really like to eat you, if only you were a little bit smaller.

Anyway, if you wanted to, the people in the Florida Everglades booth showed you how to pick up a baby alligator and hold it. If you held it right behind its jaws, it couldn't twist its head around and bite off your finger. I held one. I was really proud. They took a Polaroid picture of me holding it. I took the picture to school and showed the guys in my homeroom. Everybody was impressed—everybody but Andrew Clancy.

"You think that's a big deal?" said Andrew. "That's nothing. I went to the actual Florida Everglades and I *wrestled* an alligator—a grown-up one that was twelve feet long."

"Get out of here," I said.

~ 3 ~

"I swear," said Andrew.

"Prove it!" I said.

"I've got a picture," said Andrew.

"Bring it to school tomorrow," I said.

"I can't," said Andrew. "I lent it to my cousin Warren, who took it to France. He lost it at the Eiffel Tower."

The kids in my class are used to Andrew's bragging and lying. But Andrew was really making me mad.

"Andrew, you're so full of it," I said.

"I'm telling the truth," said Andrew.

"Prove it. Take a lie-detector test."

"Fine," said Andrew. "Do you have a lie detector?"

"No," I said, "but my dad is writing a magazine article about the police now. He's doing some interviews at a police station, and I think they have a polygraph there. Polygraph means lie detector, in case you didn't know."

By now there was a whole crowd of boys around us. Everyone was hoping Andrew Clancy might finally get caught in one of his whoppers.

"Everybody knows a polygraph is a lie detector," said Andrew. "I learned that when I was two."

"So, if my dad arranges it, you'd come to the police station and take a polygraph test?" I said.

"Sure," said Andrew.

I was amazed he agreed. But with all those kids there, he could hardly refuse.

Just then Mrs. Coleman-Levin came into the classroom. She's our homeroom teacher and our science teacher.

"Boys, I'd just like to remind you again about the Horace Hyde-White School science fair," said Mrs. Coleman-Levin. "It's next Monday. As I mentioned before, the theme will be energy, and our local electric company is offering prizes to the winners."

"What are the prizes?" asked Vernon Manteuffel. Vernon is a rich kid who's always letting you know just how rich he is. He also sweats a lot.

"First prize is one hundred dollars," said Mrs. Coleman-Levin.

We all got pretty excited about that. Everybody but Vernon, that is. He rolled his eyes. He probably gets a hundred dollars for his weekly allowance.

"Now, today is Thursday," said Mrs. Coleman-Levin. "The science fair will be on Monday, so you'll have plenty of time to finish your projects."

"What do you mean 'plenty of time'?" I said. "That's less than a week."

"You have today, which is Thursday, and tomorrow, which is Friday," said Mrs. Coleman-Levin. "And you have the whole weekend. That's plenty. And the grade you get on your science-fair project will be fifty percent of your final grade. Now, boys, we're all going to divide up. Everybody must choose a partner with whom to build his project."

"I want to work with Spencer," I said.

Spencer is my best friend. He's also the smartest kid in school. For last year's science fair, Spencer made a model of the human digestive system. He built it out of clear plastic tubing. At one end he put in a cheeseburger. At a couple places in the plastic tubing, he poured in chemicals that were just like the stomach's digestive juices. By the time the cheeseburger got to the other end of the plastic tubing, it had turned into poop. I mean, it even *smelled* like poop. The kids all loved it. The adults all thought it was gross, but they gave it first prize anyway.

"I'd like Spencer to work with some-body who needs extra help," said Mrs. Coleman-Levin. "Zack, you may choose either Vernon or Andrew."

Vernon or Andrew? What a choice! I couldn't stand either one.

"Can't I work with Stephen Tanico or Ben Lerner?" I asked.

Mrs. Coleman-Levin shook her head. She hates it when you don't do what she asks you to do.

"How about Josh Bloom or Benny Davis?" I said.

"Vernon or Andrew, Zack," she said. "Choose, or I'll choose for you."

If I didn't choose, I was positive she would make me work with Vernon Manteuffel—I really was. And I can't stand Vernon even more than I can't stand Andrew Clancy.

"OK," I said. "I choose Andrew."

If Andrew didn't brag so much, he wouldn't be such a bad kid. And he has a good imagination. If Dad could get the cops to test Andrew on a polygraph, maybe that would cut down on his bragging.

"Zack, you're lucky to be getting me as a partner," said Andrew. "You may not know this, but I come from a long line of inventors. Ancestors of mine invented the telescope, the steam engine and the whoopee cushion."

"Is that so?" I asked. "Why don't we continue this discussion when you're hooked up to the polygraph?"

Little did I know that hooking Andrew up to the polygraph might blow our entire science-fair project.

Chapter 2

The detectives at the precinct on 51st Street said it would be OK for us to see how a polygraph worked. So Dad took me and Andrew there on Thursday after school.

I don't know if you've ever been to a police station, but it's really cool. When you walk in, there's a long counter. Behind it is the desk sergeant. He's the first person you talk to.

"Excuse me, officer," said Dad. "We have an appointment with Detective Stufflebean. Is he in?"

"Upstairs," said the desk sergeant. He pointed to the stairway.

Andrew, Dad, and I walked upstairs.

Upstairs is where the detectives have their offices. A bunch of them sit at their desks, and work on cases. Detectives investigate crimes that happen in the neighborhood. They type up reports. They talk on the phone. They go out to crime scenes. They interview people who might know something about the cases. They all wear guns, either in their belts or in shoulder holsters under their arms.

"Hi, Detective Stufflebean," Dad said to a gruff-looking detective who was frowning at a report on his desk. Stufflebean looked just like all the plainclothes policemen in those old gangster movies they show on TV. His suit was kind of baggy, and his tie was loose. He was wearing a hat with a brim and it had slipped to the back of his head. A

lit cigarette hung out of the corner of his mouth.

I really hate it when people smoke around me. It makes me cough, it makes my eyes burn, and I think it's really rude. I was thinking of telling Detective Stufflebean that. But then I thought maybe I'd wait until I knew him better.

"Who are these individuals?" said Detective Stufflebean, frowning.

"This is my son, Zack, and his friend Andrew Clancy," said Dad.

We all shook hands. Detective Stufflebean was staring hard at Andrew. Andrew was staring hard at the detective's gun.

"My cousin is a detective in Long Island," said Andrew. "He's shot twelve perps."

"I sincerely doubt that," said Detective Stufflebean, frowning and smoking. He got up. "All right, gentlemen," he said. "It's time for the polygraph."

Dad, Andrew, and I followed Detective Stufflebean into a little office next door. The polygraph was on a table.

"Gentlemen, this is a polygraph," said Detective Stufflebean. "It is also known as a lie detector."

"I knew that," said Andrew. "I've got one at home. Except mine is a lot newer."

Detective Stufflebean's eyes got narrow. He stared at Andrew a few seconds, smoking, without saying anything.

"In a moment, kid," he said, "I'm going to hook you up to the polygraph. It'll measure your breathing, your blood pressure, and how much you sweat. See that roll of paper there?"

"Yes," said Andrew.

"When I turn on the machine," said the detective, "that roll of paper will start moving. Those little arms with pens attached to the ends of them will start zigzagging on the roll of paper. If you lie, the pens will zig way up, like a mountain. Then I'll know you're lying, and so will every man in this room. So will every man in this police station. You better tell the truth, kid."

"Hey, Stufflebean," another detective called. "The captain wants you in his office."

"I'll be right back," said Detective Stufflebean. "Do not, under any circumstances, touch the polygraph while I am gone."

"No problem," said Andrew. But the minute the detective left, Andrew started messing with the knobs of the polygraph.

"Andrew, what are you *doing?*" said Dad. He grabbed Andrew and pulled him away from the polygraph. "Didn't you hear what the detective told you?"

"Yeah, yeah, I heard," said Andrew. But Andrew didn't stop. "Boy," asked Andrew, "that detective is pretty grumpy, isn't he?"

"He's going to be even grumpier if you

break that polygraph, Andrew," said Dad. He pulled Andrew away again. "And *I'm* the one he's going to blame," said Dad.

Andrew stopped fooling with the polygraph just as Detective Stufflebean walked back in. The detective was still frowning. He was still smoking. There was one lit cigarette in his mouth, and another in his hand. He was also coughing. I could have told him why he was coughing, but I decided not to.

"All right, gentlemen," said the detective. "Now we can begin."

He hooked Andrew up to the machine. Wires went from Andrew's arm, chest, and fingers to the polygraph. The detective turned a switch and the roll of paper started moving. Suddenly, there was a soft popping sound and a shower of sparks.

"Did anybody touch this machine while I was gone?" asked the detective. "Answer yes or no."

"No way," said Andrew.

Dad rolled his eyes.

The pens on the roll of paper went crazy, zigzagging all over the place. "Kid," said the detective to Andrew, "did you touch the polygraph while I was gone? Answer yes or no."

"No," said Andrew.

The pens went crazy again.

"OK, kid," said Detective Stufflebean, "let's start over. To show you what happens when you're telling the truth, I'm going to ask you some questions we already know the answers to. First, is your name Andrew Clancy? Answer yes or no."

"Yes," said Andrew.

The pens hardly zigged at all.

"Are you in the fifth grade, Mr. Clancy? Answer yes or no."

"Yes," said Andrew.

The pens hardly zigged.

"See how the pens hardly moved when I asked your name and grade?" said the detective. "That's what happens when you tell the truth. Next question: Do you have a detective who's a cousin on Long Island, Mr. Clancy? Answer yes or no."

"Yes," said Andrew.

The pens still didn't zig.

"Next question: Did your cousin shoot twelve perpetrators?" said the detective. "Answer yes or no."

"Yes," said Andrew.

The pens went crazy. There were sparks from the machine. And there was a sound like cloth ripping. That sound didn't come from the machine.

"Kid, you just split your pants," said Detective Stufflebean.

Dad and I looked at Andrew's pants. They were split, just like the detective said. Weirdly, Andrew's butt looked bigger.

How could it have suddenly split his pants?

"I'm going to ask you again, Mr. Clancy," said Detective Stufflebean. "Did you touch the polygraph while I was gone? Answer yes or no."

"No," said Andrew.

Again, the pens went crazy. Again, I heard cloth ripping. *Wow!* Andrew's butt *had* gotten bigger. You could see his underpants. They had clowns and balloons.

"Andrew," I said, "I think your butt is growing every time you lie."

"You're crazy," said Andrew.

"No, I'm not," I said. "Remember Pinocchio? His nose got longer every time he told a lie. You're just like Pinocchio, only with a different body part."

"Kid," said Detective Stufflebean, "I got a good mind to take you into the interrogation room and *make* you tell me the truth."

"Excuse me, Detective Stufflebean," said

Dad. "Aren't you being a little too tough on this boy? He's only ten years old."

"Too tough?" said Detective Stufflebean. "Let me tell you something, mister. Lying to a cop is serious business, see? Lying to a cop goes against everything this country stands for. Lying to a cop is like lying to George Washington or Babe Ruth or the Grand Canyon. I've sent people up the river to Sing Sing Prison for lying to a cop."

"OK, that's enough," said Dad. "We're going home."

"Whatever you say," said the detective. He pulled the polygraph wires off Andrew.

"Just out of curiosity, kid," said Detective Stufflebean. "What kind of cases does your detective cousin work on?"

"Homicide," said Andrew.

"Homicide, eh?" said Detective Stufflebean. "No kidding."

"Yeah," said Andrew. "Sometimes when

he's stuck on a case, he calls to ask my advice. I often give him leads that end up cracking cases. In fact, I've solved so many homicide cases for him, the Long Island Police made me an honorary detective. They gave me a real detective's badge."

R-R-R-R-I-I-I-P-P-P!

I heard another ripping sound. Although Andrew wasn't hooked up to the polygraph now, his butt was starting to pop out of his underpants. It was the grossest thing I'd ever seen. Dad put his raincoat over Andrew and we hurried out of the room and started down the stairs.

"That kid has major problems with the truth," said Detective Stufflebean, frowning, smoking, and coughing.

For me and Andrew, our major problems had only begun.

Chapter 3

On Friday, Andrew came to school wearing a huge pair of sweatpants. I was the only one who knew why. He was trying to hide the size of his enormous butt.

"Hey, Andrew," said Vernon Manteuffel. "Why are your sweatpants so baggy?"

"Because," said Andrew, "my sweatpants are in the laundry. I had to wear my dad's."

"Yeah?" asked Vernon. "Are you wearing your dad's butt, too?"

Some of the kids laughed.

"Hey, Andrew," said Stephen Tanico.

"You've sure got a lot of junk in your trunk."

More kids laughed. Mrs. Coleman-Levin told us to be quiet. She said to start working with our partners on our science projects. Andrew and I tried to think of a project we could do. I couldn't help staring at his butt.

"Hey, Zack," said Andrew. "Are you staring at my butt?"

"Uh, no," I said. Then I remembered what telling lies was doing to Andrew. "Well, yeah," I said.

"Why are you staring at my butt?"

"Because of how big it's grown," I said. "Haven't you noticed?"

"It may be a little bigger, yeah," said Andrew. "But that's because I've been doing special butt exercises. I want my butt to grow even bigger. I want to be able to sit on people and flatten them like a Japanese sumo wrestler. My butt could become a lethal weapon."

"It will if you keep on telling lies," I said. "This all started at the police station when you were hooked up to the polygraph. Every time you told a lie, your butt got bigger."

"We're not here to talk about my butt," said Andrew. "We're here to talk about our science project, OK?"

"OK," I said. "So? Do you have any ideas?"

"Well, this is supposed to have something to do with energy, right?"

"Right," I said.

"OK," said Andrew. "I've been reading that they're experimenting with using left-over stuff from fast-food restaurants as fuel. Old chicken fat and old cooking oil left over from making french fries."

"Yeah, I heard something about that," I said.

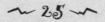

"So why don't we go to all the McDonald's and Burger Kings we can find and collect two gallons of old cooking oil from french fries. We put one gallon of gasoline in *my* dad's car. We put one gallon of old french-fry cooking oil in *your* dad's car. Then our dads drive both cars around the block till one of them runs out of fuel. We videotape the whole thing and show it at the science fair. "

"Why does the french fries oil have to go in *my* dad's car?" I said.

"Because *my* dad would *kill* me if I put it in *his* car," said Andrew.

We thought some more.

Vernon strolled over to where we were sitting. I thought he was trying to spy on us.

"Yes, Vernon?" I said. "Was there something you wanted?"

"I just wanted to see what your science project is going to be," said Vernon. "Because Stephen and I came up with something so cool you won't even believe it."

"Our project is going to be way cooler than yours," I said.

"Really?" said Vernon. "What is it?"

"If you think I'm going to tell you now, Manteuffel, when you could steal it, you're crazy," I said.

Vernon laughed. "You and Andrew can't think of anything, can you?" he said. "Why don't you build something to measure people's butts?"

"Why don't you get your butt out of here?" I said.

The idea Andrew and I finally came up with was maybe not as interesting as making fuel out of old cooking oil, but it was a whole lot more practical. We decided to take a two-seater bicycle and hook it up to a small generator. When both of us got on the seats and pedaled really fast, I figured it might generate enough electricity to light up some light bulbs.

On Saturday we went out and searched the yard sales and secondhand stores. Andrew was walking a little funny now. His butt was so big, he was more waddling than walking.

We bought an old two-seater bicycle. We bought an old generator. We bought a whole bunch of bulbs and arranged them on a board to spell out words. We attached the board with the bulbs on a pipe over our heads. We hooked up wires between the bike and the generator, and between the generator and the sign. The bulbs on the sign spelled out ZACK AND ANDREW RULE!

It took a lot of work, but we finished our project by Sunday night, the day before the science fair. It was so cool, I actually thought we might have a shot at winning that hundred bucks.

There was just one problem. By Sunday, Andrew had told a lot of lies. He told the man who sold us the two-seater bicycle that we were in training for the Tour de France bike race in France. He told the girl at the lightbulb store that he was the great-great-great grandson of Thomas Edison, the inventor of the lightbulb. Stuff like that. He just couldn't stop.

And every time Andrew told a lie, his butt grew bigger. It was so big now that, if it got any bigger, it wasn't going to fit on the bike seat anymore. And if Andrew's butt didn't fit on his bike seat, Andrew couldn't pedal, which meant our project was doomed.

Chapter 4

It was Monday, the day of the science fair. I called Andrew before school to make sure his butt hadn't grown any bigger.

"No," he said. "It's the same size as when you left here yesterday."

Even through the phone I could hear a ripping noise. It was probably Andrew's sweatpants. I had no time to lose.

"Listen to me, Andrew," I said. "Just leave for school right now. And don't talk to anybody on the way." If he didn't talk to anybody, he couldn't lie, I figured.

By the time Dad dropped me off at school with the bike and the generator, the gym was crowded with kids. It was so loud you could hardly hear yourself think. All the kids were setting up their science projects and yelling instructions to each other. I went to take a look at some of the projects.

The first few I saw looked pretty stupid.

There was a scale model of the Space Shuttle, powered by a bottle rocket. While setting it up, the boys who built it accidentally set off the bottle rocket. The Space Shuttle was now embedded in the ceiling of the gym.

There was an automatic umbrella that opened and closed with the push of a button. This one was powered by solar energy. Of course, on rainy days it wouldn't be sunny enough to power it. It wasn't very practical.

There was a burglar alarm. It attached to

the windows of a house. If a burglar tried to open a window from the outside at night, a fake monster with a horrible face would pop up from behind a bush and make a shrieking noise. Unfortunately, this also happened if somebody opened the window during the day or from inside the house.

Because Spencer is so smart, I figured he'd be our biggest competition. I dreaded to see what he'd come up with. I walked over to where Spencer and his partner Wendell Perkins were putting together something really complicated. It had wires and stuff all over the place.

"Spencer," I said, "what *is* that?"

"It's a device for measuring the amount of energy you use when you do various activities," Spencer said.

"Like what?" I said.

"Like eating a taco or playing a video

game or tying your shoes," he said. "It's really fantastic. You just hook these wires up to the person you're testing."

"Kind of like a polygraph?" I said.

"Kind of like a polygraph," Spencer said. "Only you have to hook it up to a lot more places than a polygraph. You put two wires on each side of the forehead. You put one in each ear. You put one on each wrist. You put one on each ankle. You put one up each nostril..."

"Uh-huh," I said. "Tell me, Spencer, do you think anybody is going to agree to put wires up their nostrils?"

Spencer sighed.

"I don't know, Zack," he said. "Unfortunately, the wires that go up the nostrils are the most important ones. They measure the amount of oxygen the person uses."

"Without them," said Wendell, "we don't know if it's going to work."

Hmmm. It sounded to me as though Spencer had designed a science project that might not even get tested, which meant that Spencer and Wendell weren't much of a threat.

I went over to look at Vernon's project. His partner was Stephen Tanico. They had a lot of electronic stuff wired together. A CD player. A tape deck. Lots of speakers. I mean *lots* of speakers. There were some speakers that were bigger than refrigerators.

"You know how powerful that speaker is?" said Vernon, pointing. "When I turn up the volume it'll shatter windows a block away. It'll shatter the lenses of anybody wearing glasses in the entire building."

"Unless you're wearing earplugs," said Stephen Tanico, "it'll shatter your eardrums."

"So this is your project?" I said. "A

really loud stereo system that breaks glass and makes people deaf?"

"Isn't it great?" said Stephen.

"So what did you do—just go out and buy a lot of expensive stereo components?" I said.

"No, you moron," said Vernon. "We also hooked them *up*. You think it's easy hooking up all those speakers?"

"Right," I said.

"So what's *your* project?" Vernon asked.

"You'll see," I said.

A few minutes later Andrew slowly lumbered into the gym with the rest of our stuff. Had his butt grown? Oh, yes! If it got any bigger and it would be dragging on the floor.

"Andrew," I said, "I'm starting to think we've got a really good chance of winning. Come on. Let's get on the bike and practice."

We set up the bike, got on, and started to pedal. Andrew had a lot of trouble keeping his butt on the seat. It was hanging over the seat on all sides. We pedaled, but the bulbs didn't light up.

"Pedal faster, Andrew," I said.

"I'm trying, Zack," he said. "But it's hard."

"It probably wouldn't be so hard if your butt wasn't so huge," I said.

"What?"

"Never mind."

I pedaled twice as hard to make up for Andrew. It wasn't helping. Along came Vernon.

"Is that your project?" said Vernon. "A stationary bike? What's the point of a stationary bike?"

"It lights up a sign, you moron," I said.

"We're going to win," said Andrew. "A few minutes ago, two of the judges passed

by. I overheard one of them. He said our project was the most brilliant one he'd ever seen."

Oh, no! It was as if a bike tire pump was attached to Andrew and was blowing up his butt. You could actually see it expanding.

Vernon was staring at Andrew.

"Andrew, did you know your butt just got bigger?" Vernon asked.

Andrew laughed.

"Zack says my butt grows bigger whenever I lie," said Andrew. "Just like Pinocchio's nose grew longer. But that's ridiculous, because I— "

"Andrew! Don't say another word!" I commanded.

"—never lie," said Andrew, finishing his sentence.

It was too late. There was a slight ripping sound. Andrew's butt had just outgrown another pair of sweatpants.

"I hate to say it," said Vernon, "but Zack is right."

Oh, no! Soon Andrew's butt would be too big to fit on the bicycle seat.

Andrew slowly pulled himself off the seat and started walking away.

"Andrew," I said, "the judging is going to start soon. Where are you going?"

"To the john," said Andrew.

"I'll come with you," said Vernon.

I suddenly realized what Vernon might be up to. He saw that Andrew's butt was almost too big for the bike. Vernon was going to egg on Andrew to brag and lie until he couldn't get on the bike at all. Then we'd lose for sure.

"I'm coming, too," I said.

Chapter 5

Andrew was in the bathroom stall with the door closed. Vernon was standing outside.

"You know, Andrew," said Vernon, "at home, my personal bathroom is huge. It's got mirrored walls and a mirrored ceiling. And my bathtub has a Jacuzzi."

"Keep quiet, Andrew! Don't say a word!" I shouted. But Andrew couldn't be stopped.

"Big deal," said Andrew. "My bathroom has a sauna and a forty-eight-inch TV in the wall. Uh-oh."

"What's wrong, Andrew?" I asked.

"Uh, my butt seems to have gotten too big for the toilet seat," said Andrew.

Vernon had an evil grin on his face. I heard Andrew's toilet flush.

"Andrew, listen to me," I said. "If you don't stop lying right now, your butt will grow so big it'll burst right out of this building. It'll get as big as a mountain. Snow drifts will pile up at the top. Guides will lead expeditions up to the top of your butt. Skiers will ski down it!"

"Andrew," said Vernon with a nasty smile, "in my bathroom I have a refrigerator stocked with Cokes, and a freezer stocked with frozen Kit Kat bars."

"Andrew, cover your ears! Don't answer him!" I shouted.

I heard Andrew sigh. I knew he was trying not to answer. I knew he no longer had any control over his bragging.

"In *my* bathroom," said Andrew, "I have

a brick pizza oven and a guy who can make me pizza or calzones twenty-four hours a day. I can stay in my bathroom for two weeks without coming out."

The stall door was unlocked and opened only an inch.

"Uh-oh," said Andrew. "I can't get out. I'm stuck."

Vernon cackled and clapped his hands.

"Oh, what a shame," he said.

I had seen this coming. Unless I could get Andrew out of the stall, our chances of winning anything at the science fair had just gone right down the toilet.

"Andrew, listen to me," I said. "I'm going for help. While I'm gone, promise you won't say a single word to Vernon. Do you promise?"

"I promise," said Andrew.

I went to get Floyd Hogmeister, our school janitor. He was sitting in his

basement office, working on a toilet flusher.

"Mr. Hogmeister," I said. "We have an emergency. We need your help."

"What's the problem?" said Floyd.

"It's Andrew Clancy," I said. "His butt is growing."

"My butt is growing, too," said Floyd. "It happens as you get older."

"No," I said, "this is different. Andrew's butt is growing about an inch a second. It's so big now, he can't get out of the bathroom stall."

"Oh, why didn't you say so?" said Floyd.

He got his tool kit. He also picked up a crowbar and a can of axle grease.

"What's with the crowbar and the axle grease?" I asked.

"I'll have him grease himself up so he's good and slippery," said Floyd. "Then I'll pry him out of there with my crowbar."

"That's not going to work," I said.

Floyd looked offended.

"You sure?" he asked.

"I'm sure," I said.

"Then I can't help him," said Floyd. He went back to working on his toilet flusher.

I ran back upstairs. Mrs. Coleman-Levin spotted me in the hallway and hurried over.

"Zack!" she said. "Where have you and Andrew been? The judging for the science fair is about to start. I've been trying to convince the judges to postpone the start, but they're getting quite impatient."

"Mrs. Coleman-Levin, we have an emergency," I said. "Andrew's butt is too big to get out of the john."

"How on earth did it get that big?" she asked.

"Well, every time he tells a lie, his butt grows bigger," I said. "I guess he just told one lie too many. I asked Floyd Hogmeister to help us, but that wasn't any good. He wanted Andrew to grease himself up with axle grease. Then he thought he could pry Andrew out with a crowbar."

"No no," said Mrs. Coleman-Levin. "Axle grease and crowbars *never* work in cases of lies and butt growth."

"Then what does?" I asked.

"Truth serum," she said.

"Truth serum?" I repeated.

"Also known as sodium pentothal. It sometimes gets criminals to tell the truth. Truth serum is the only way," she said. "Unfortunately, I can't think of a place where you could possibly get any fast."

"*I* can," I said. "I'll be right back. Try to hold the judges a few more minutes!"

I went to the pay phone in the hallway. I called Information and got the number of the 51st Street precinct. Then I called the police station and asked for Detective Stufflebean. Pretty soon he got on the line.

"Detective Stufflebean," I said, "this is Zack. My dad and I visited you last Thursday with my friend Andrew."

"The kid whose caboose got bigger every time he told a lie," said Detective Stufflebean.

"Right," I said. "The thing is, sir, we're having an emergency here at school. Andrew's told so many lies that his butt is too big to get out of the toilet stall. If we can't get him out right away, we're going to have to drop out of the science fair." I paused. "Would you happen to have any truth serum over there?"

"Truth serum?" said the detective. "Sure. Why?"

"Well," I said, "I think Andrew would like to start telling the truth now. But he needs a head start. If you could possibly come over here and give him some truth serum, I think it would do the trick."

"Tell me something," Detective Stufflebean said. "How serious is he about wanting to stop lying?"

"Very serious," I said. "Well...pretty serious, at least."

I heard Detective Stufflebean take a long puff on his cigarette. I thought of mentioning how dangerous it was to smoke. I figured it wasn't the right moment to tell him.

"You wouldn't lie to a cop, now, would you, son?" he asked.

"Sir, I'm not the guy who has problems with the truth," I said.

"OK, I'll tell you what," said Detective Stufflebean. "I'll come to your school with the truth serum. But you kids better not be lying to me."

"Thank you, Detective Stufflebean," I said. "And please—hurry! Use your flashing red lights and your siren."

I gave Detective Stufflebean the school's

address and went back to the bathroom to wait.

"Andrew, it's Zack. I'm back. Help is on the way. Detective Stufflebean is bringing truth serum."

"Truth serum?" Andrew said. "What do I need with that?"

"It's the only thing that works in cases of lies and butt growth," I said.

"Andrew," Vernon taunted, "in my bedroom I have a water bed that's so big it has a wave-making machine."

"Vernon, shut up!" I shouted. "Andrew, don't answer him!"

"I'm trying not to," Andrew called, "but I can't hold out much longer."

"Just try to hang in there," I pleaded.

Detective Stufflebean must have really hurried. He arrived about five minutes later. He was breathing hard from running. He was carrying a small black leather case.

"OK," said the detective. "Where's the boy with the giant labonza?"

"Right there in that stall." I pointed. "Andrew, Detective Stufflebean is here with the truth serum!"

"Goody," Andrew said. He didn't sound all that happy.

Detective Stufflebean opened his black leather case. He took out a small glass bottle. He poured the serum in the bottle into a paper cup. Then he leaned over the door of the toilet stall and gave it to Andrew.

Vernon shook his head and left the bathroom in disgust.

"I drank it," Andrew said, "but let me tell you—that stuff tastes awful."

"OK, kid," Detective Stufflebean said. "The truth serum might already be working. Let's begin. Do you have a cousin who's a detective in Long Island? Answer yes or no."

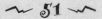

"OK. Yes," Andrew said. "I *do* have a cousin in Long Island. And yes, he *is* a detective." Andrew paused. "But I have to tell you—he never shot twelve perps. He never shot anybody at all. And I have to tell you—I never solved a homicide case for him. And the Long Island Police Department never gave me a detective's badge."

"Good, Andrew," I said. "Way to go!"

"And I did mess around with the polygraph in the police station," said Andrew. "And I don't have a better one at home."

Detective Stufflebean nodded. He was still frowning, but he almost smiled.

"Good, Andrew," I said. "Go on. What about your bathroom?"

"I have to tell you—I don't have a sauna in my bathroom," said Andrew. "And I don't have a forty-eight-inch TV in the wall there either."

"Good," I said. "And what about the brick pizza oven?"

"I have to tell you—I don't have a brick pizza oven in my bathroom,"Andrew said. "And I don't have a guy who can make me pizza or calzone twenty-four hours a day. And the longest I ever stayed in my bathroom was an hour and a half. Hey!"

"What is it?" I asked.

"My butt," Andrew said. "It's shrinking! It's shrinking big-time!"

"Andrew, pull up your pants!" I shouted. "If we hurry, we can just make it back to the gym for the judging!"

Then we ran out of the bathroom.

"Thank you, Detective Stufflebean," I called after me.

"And stop smoking!" Andrew shouted as we headed for the gym. "It's killing you. That's the honest truth!"

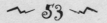

Chapter 6

We raced into the gym. Andrew's butt had shrunk so much, his dad's sweatpants no longer fit him. He had to hold them at his waist to keep them from falling down.

When we got back to our stationary bike, the judges from the Board of Education were already waiting. One of the judges was a man in a dark blue suit. He had a fake-looking wig on his head. The other judge was a heavy-set woman in a black dress. She had a wart on her nose.

"We thought you weren't coming," said

the female judge. "We were just going to mark you disqualified."

"Well, we had a slight emergency in the bathroom," I said.

"My butt got so big from telling lies, I couldn't get out of the john," said Andrew.

Both judges frowned. I shot Andrew a look to shut him up, but he didn't catch it. It was obvious the truth serum was still working on him.

"I have to tell you—my butt got so big, it popped right out of my pants," said Andrew.

The woman judge started to say something, but I interrupted.

"Anyway," I said loudly, "now we're here, and we're ready to show our project."

"Then go ahead," said the male judge.

We got on the bike. We climbed onto the bike seats. Andrew was in front, I was just behind him. We started pedaling. For some reason, the sign wasn't lighting up.

"Excuse me, sir," Andrew said to the male judge. "I couldn't help noticing your hair. I really have to tell you—that wig doesn't look real at all."

"What?" said the man. His face had turned bright red.

"Andrew, shut up!" I said.

"I'm really sorry, sir," said Andrew, "but I have to tell you—it looks like a skunk dropped dead on your head."

"Pedal, Andrew!" I shouted. "Shut up and pedal!"

We both pedaled as hard as we could.

The sign above our heads lit up, brighter than ever before: ZACK AND ANDREW RULE! it said.

Andrew leaned toward the woman judge.

"Excuse me," said Andrew. "I have to tell you—my grandpa had a wart on his nose, too. But his doctor removed it. He looks much better now. I could find out the name of the doctor for you."

The woman's face turned purple.

I reached in front of me and clapped my hand over Andrew's mouth.

"Stop talking and pedal!"

~~~

The judges were pretty mad. I told them about Andrew's problem and about the truth serum, and they calmed down. But not calm enough to give us any prizes, of course.

So we didn't win the hundred bucks. But neither did Spencer and Wendell. And neither did Vernon and Stephen. The project that won first prize was...a battery tester. A *battery* tester! Can you believe that?

By the time the fair was over, the truth serum had worn off. And I'm glad to say that Andrew seemed pretty grateful for all I'd done.

"Zack," he said, "I know I brag a lot. And I know I'm a pain in the butt. But I really want to thank you."

"You're welcome, Andrew," I said. "I just hope the whole thing has taught you something."

"It certainly has," he said. "I also want to let you know that I was really impressed with that Polaroid you showed me. The one of you holding the baby alligator."

"Well, thank you, Andrew," I said. "I appreciate that. And I guess you never wrestled a grown-up twelve-foot-long alligator in the Everglades, did you?"

"No," said Andrew. "I didn't."

"I didn't think so," I said.

"It was actually a crocodile," said Andrew.

THE ZACK FILES™

OUT-OF-THIS-WORLD FAN CLUB!

Looking for even more info on all the strange, otherworldly happenings going on in *The Zack Files*? Get the inside scoop by becoming a member of *The Zack Files* Out-Of-This-World Fan Club! Just send in the form below and we'll send you your *Zack Files* Out-Of-This-World Fan Club kit including an official fan club membership card, a really cool *Zack Files* magnet, and a newsletter featuring excerpts from Zack's upcoming paranormal adventures, supernatural news from around the world, puzzles, and more! And as a member you'll continue to receive the newsletter six times a year! The best part is- it's all free!

✄ ---

☐ Yes! I want to check out *The Zack Files*
  Out-Of-This-World Fan Club!

name: _____ age: ____

address: _____

city/town: _____ state: ___ zip: _____

Send this form to: Penguin Putnam Books for
                       Young Readers
                       Mass Merchandise Marketing
                       Dept. ZACK
                       345 Hudson Street
                       New York, NY 10014

What else happens to Zack?
Find out in

Just Add Water...
and Scream!

I tore open the packet. I poured the spores into another bowl. Each spore had two little dark spots on it, like eyes. It was almost as if they were staring at me. That really creeped me out.

"Go ahead," said Spencer. "Add water."

"Uh, okay," I said.

Staring at the spores, I carried the bowl toward the sink. I turned on the faucet and added water. The instant the water hit the spores, I heard a weird hissing sound. Then—and I swear this is the truth—I thought I heard them burp.

I screamed.